THE LEPRECHAUN
in the Basement

KATHY TUCKER

illustrations by JOHN SANDFORD

Albert Whitman & Company

Morton Grove, Illinois

The artist would like to thank those people, large and small, who helped in the making of this book: Cody Hacker, Kathy Hacker, Chuck Hacker, Chas Hacker, Elmer Elf, and Eleanor Sandford.

Library of Congress Cataloging-in-Publication Data
Tucker, Kathy.
The leprechaun in the basement /by Kathy Tucker; illustrated by John Sandford.
p. cm.
Summary: After encountering a leprechaun, Michael McKeever asks him to help with his family's money problems, but unable to part with his gold, the wee man finds another way to help.
ISBN 0-8075-4450-7
[1. Leprechauns—Fiction. 2. Shoes—Fiction.]
I. Sandford, John, 1953– ill.
II. Title.
PZ7.T82255Lg 1999
[Fic]—dc21   98-9318
CIP
AC

Text copyright © 1999 by Kathleen Tucker Brooks.
Illustrations copyright © 1999 by John Sandford.
Published in 1999 by Albert Whitman & Company,
6340 Oakton Street, Morton Grove, Illinois 60053-2723.
Published simultaneously in Canada by General Publishing, Limited, Toronto.
Printed in the United States of America.
10 9 8 7 6 5

The illustrations are done in watercolor and pencil.
The design is by Scott Piehl.

Albert Whitman & Company is also the publisher of The Boxcar Children® Mysteries.
For more information about all our fine books, visit us at www.awhitmanco.com.

For my dear Aunt Peg,
and with thanks to the Kearneys,
McKeevers, O'Learys, and Bennetts.
— K. T.

For George Brunskill.
— J. S.

O'Leary was a leprechaun.

A long time ago he had come from Ireland stowed in a trunk. Now he lived in the basement of a house in Chicago.

He led a quiet life. Sometimes he read the newspapers in the recycling bin. Most of the time he just sat by his pot of gold coins, polishing them.

He loved his gold; still, once in a while he felt a little bored.

He thought that when he lived in Ireland he used to do something else, but he couldn't remember what. Perhaps I'm just getting old, he would say to himself, for although leprechauns never die, they do get older.

Michael McKeever was the boy who lived in that house, though he didn't know O'Leary was there.

It was Saint Patrick's Day. That meant it was almost spring, almost time for baseball season to begin.

Michael pulled his last year's baseball shoes from under the bed. He tried them on. His big toes jammed against the ends. The soles had begun to peel away.

Michael's heart sank. He couldn't play ball in these shoes, but how could he ask his mom and dad for new ones?

For the McKeevers were down on their luck. Michael's dad had lost his job at the computer company, and Michael's mom said they had to Make Do.

Every day Mr. McKeever searched for another job; at night, he came home looking sad and plunked himself in front of the TV. He never said, "Hey, Mike, let's go out and throw a few," the way he used to.

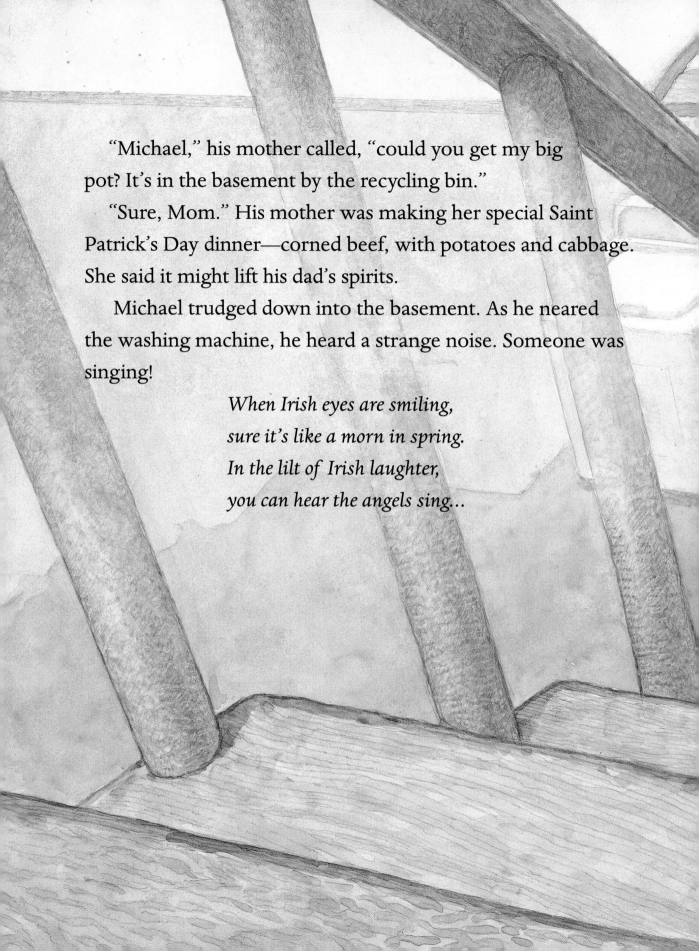

"Michael," his mother called, "could you get my big pot? It's in the basement by the recycling bin."

"Sure, Mom." His mother was making her special Saint Patrick's Day dinner—corned beef, with potatoes and cabbage. She said it might lift his dad's spirits.

Michael trudged down into the basement. As he neared the washing machine, he heard a strange noise. Someone was singing!

When Irish eyes are smiling,
sure it's like a morn in spring.
In the lilt of Irish laughter,
you can hear the angels sing...

Michael peeked around the furnace.
There in the recycling bin was a tiny old
man. He jumped up and stared at Michael.

Michael blinked. The little man looked
exactly like the pictures of the wee folk
he'd seen in a book about Ireland.

"Are you a *leprechaun?*" he asked.

O'Leary scowled—he had a bit of a
temper. "Well, I'm not from outer space!"

Michael pointed to a bowl with something sparkling in it. "What's that?" he asked.

"My gold, of course."

"Michael, I'm waiting!" his mother called.

"Coming, Ma!" Michael grabbed his mother's pot. "I'll be back," he whispered to the leprechaun.

"I was afraid of that," muttered O'Leary.

Because suddenly he knew his life would never be the same again.

At supper, Michael's dad just picked at his corned beef and cabbage. Michael could hardly eat, either. He couldn't wait to talk to the leprechaun again. But after the dishes were washed, his father went down to the basement to check on the hot water tank, and there was no chance.

In bed, Michael couldn't sleep. A leprechaun with a pot of gold—why, that gold could buy all sorts of things! The hot water tank wasn't working right, his mom's bike was broken, and he—he needed baseball shoes. He *had* to have new baseball shoes.

A leprechaun in the basement—maybe their luck was going to change.

O'Leary was awake, too. He had always liked to sing an Irish song on Saint Patrick's Day, but he could see that he had been very foolish. Now a human being knew where he was. Now there would be trouble. For humans wanted just one thing from leprechauns—they wanted gold.

The next day, Michael raced home from school. His folks weren't home yet, so the coast was clear.

The leprechaun was waiting.

"Listen," said Michael, "my dad lost his job and the hot water tank isn't working and my mom's bike is broken and I need... baseball shoes."

He held out his old shoes.

"'Tis a pity," said O'Leary. "But what can *I* do?"

"You could give us some gold."

O'Leary sighed. "Could you give up playing baseball?"

Michael shook his head. "No way! I love baseball!"

"You're a smart lad. Then you understand why leprechauns cannot give up their gold."

"But that doesn't make sense—you have so much!"

"Some things don't make sense," said O'Leary, "and still they are true."

"Leprechauns are supposed to be lucky," Michael protested.

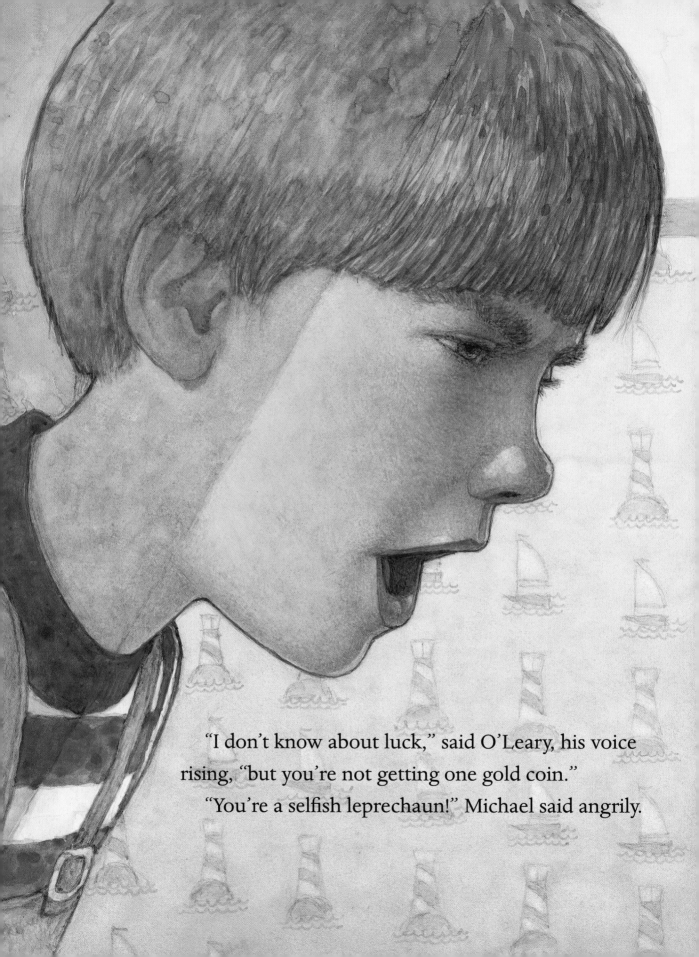

"I don't know about luck," said O'Leary, his voice rising, "but you're not getting one gold coin."

"You're a selfish leprechaun!" Michael said angrily.

O'Leary stomped his foot.

"And *you* are a greedy human being!"

Michael stalked upstairs. His father was coming in the door.

"Dad, why are we so unlucky?" he blurted out. He wasn't supposed to worry his father, but he couldn't help it; he almost felt like crying.

His father stared at him. "I guess you must think you are unlucky, with such a gloomy dad."

He put his arm around his son. "Listen—when I woke up today, I had the strongest feeling—our luck is going to change! It doesn't make sense, but it's true. I *know* we McKeevers are going to be okay. Now, let's go out and throw a few."

Like magic, Michael's spirits lifted. He ran to get his ball.

That night in bed, Michael thought about what the leprechaun had said. He didn't want to be a greedy human being.

He would Make Do. Maybe he could tape up the soles and—he reached under the bed for his shoes. Then he remembered: he had left them in the basement.

In the basement, O'Leary paced back and forth. *Was* he a selfish leprechaun?

He stared at the baseball shoes. The stitching was poorly done; the soles were made of the cheapest leather. He looked for the shoemaker's name, but there was only a tag too worn to read. Sure and begorra I could have made a better shoe myself, he thought. Why, I was the best cobbler in County Cork!

And that was how O'Leary remembered what he used to do in Ireland.

The next morning, when Michael McKeever stretched
in bed, he felt something heavy on his legs. He sat up.
There on the blanket was the most beautiful pair
of baseball shoes he had ever seen. They were green,
with excellent thick soles and good gripping spikes.
On the toes were tiny gold shamrocks.